A Fine Mouse Band

Written and illustrated by
CYNDY SZEKERES

A GOLDEN BOOK • NEW YORK

Western Publishing Company, Inc., Racine, Wisconsin 53404

Mother Mouse is busy painting.

Father Mouse is busy, too.
He needs his little mice
to help him.

Tiny fetches nails.

Brother carries some wood.
Sister finds some ribbon,
some wire, and a walnut shell.

They work all morning with Father.

Then they help him make lunch.
Tiny gets the basket of berries.
Brother carries the juice.
Sister sets the table.

After lunch, Mother shows them
her painting.
   It is beautiful!

Tiny wants to paint.
Mother helps him.
Baby watches.

Sister and Brother
work with Father.

Plink! Boomp! Clack, clackity, clack!
They are all finished.
Father and the little ones make music.

Father plunks a walnut banjo.
Sister boomps the drum.

Brother and Tiny clack the clackers.
Mother sings and Baby claps.
What a fine mouse band!

Sister and Brother start supper.

Father and Tiny take care of Baby.

Mother paints.
She puts hearts on Father's banjo.
She paints stars on Sister's drum,
and zigzagging lines on the clackers.

Plunk! Boomp! Clackity, clackity!
Tra la la, clap, clap!
A fine mouse band
marches to the supper table.

By the way, her name is Sweetie.